This item is supported in whole or part by the Institute of Museum and Library Services through the Library Services and Technology Act, administered by the Oregon State Library.

INSTITUTE of Museum and Library SERVICES

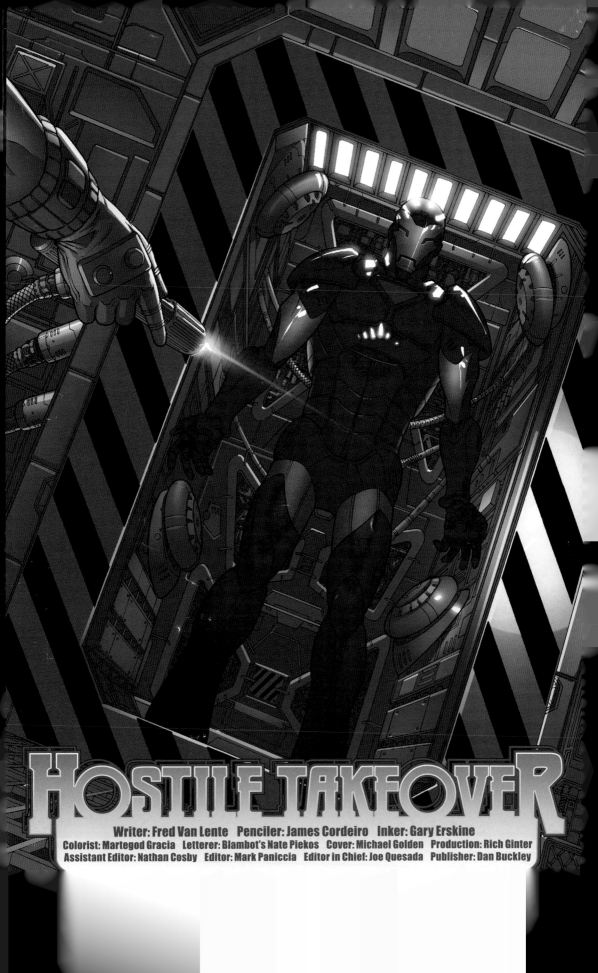

HOSTILE TAKEOVER

Writer: Fred Van Lente   Penciler: James Cordeiro   Inker: Gary Erskine
Colorist: Martegod Gracia   Letterer: Blambot's Nate Piekos   Cover: Michael Golden   Production: Rich Ginter
Assistant Editor: Nathan Cosby   Editor: Mark Paniccia   Editor in Chief: Joe Quesada   Publisher: Dan Buckley

VISIT US AT
www.abdopublishing.com

Reinforced library bound edition published in 2009 by Spotlight, a division of the ABDO Publishing Group, 8000 West 78th Street, Edina, Minnesota 55439. Spotlight produces high-quality reinforced library bound editions for schools and libraries. Published by agreement with Marvel Characters, Inc.

Printed in the United States of America, North Mankato, Minnesota.
012009
062012

Library of Congress Cataloging-in-Publication Data

Van Lente, Fred.
  Hostile takeover / Fred Van Lente, writer ; James Cordeiro, penciler ; Gary Erskine, inker ; Martegod Gracia, colorist ; Nate Piekos, letterer. -- Reinforced library bound ed.
     p. cm. -- (Iron Man)
  "Marvel."
  ISBN 978-1-59961-554-7
  1. Graphic novels. [1. Graphic novels.] I. Cordeiro, James, ill. II. Title.
  PZ7.7.V26Hos 2008
  741.5'973--dc22

                                        2008000107

All Spotlight books have reinforced library bindings and are manufactured in the United States of America.

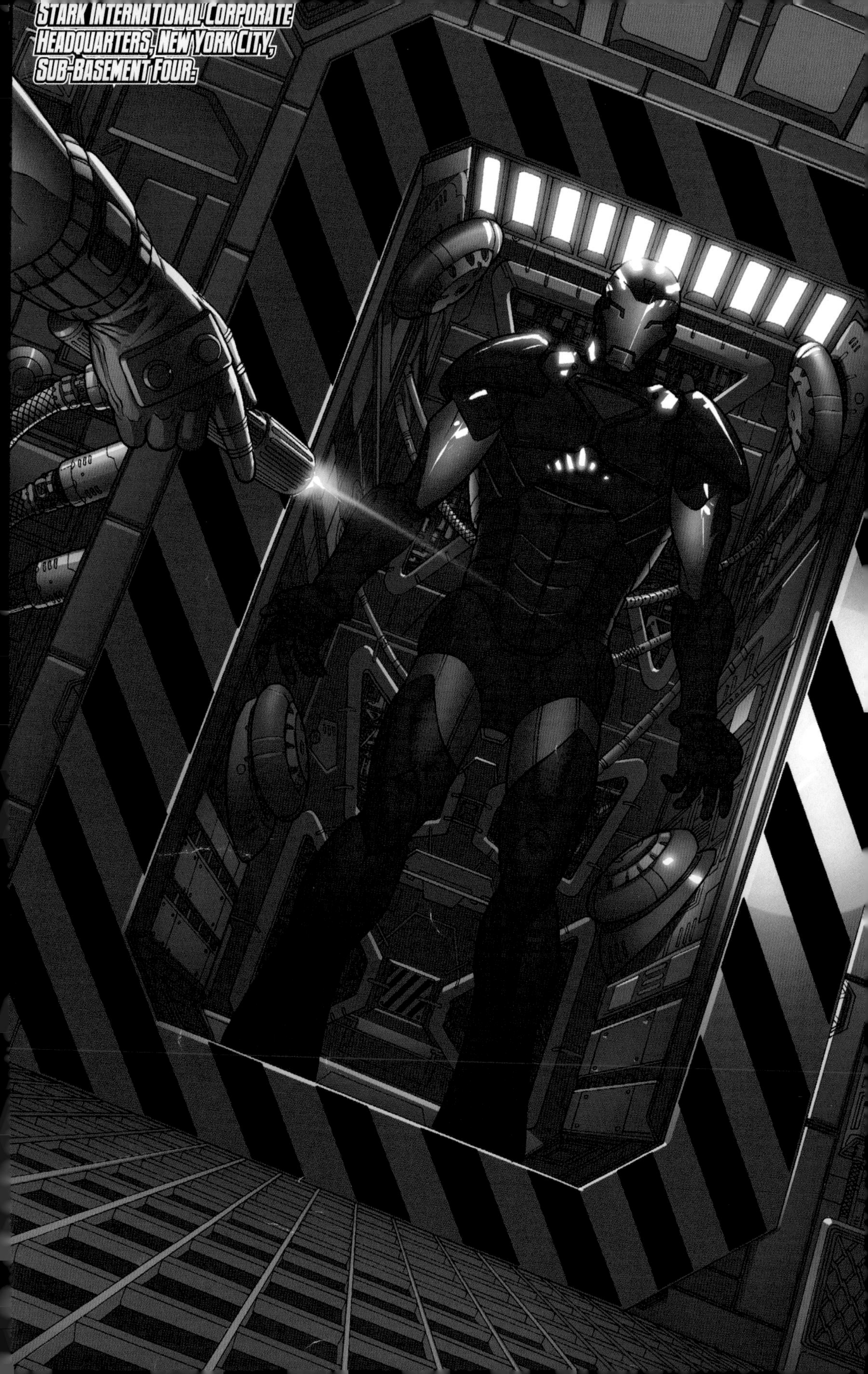
STARK INTERNATIONAL CORPORATE HEADQUARTERS, NEW YORK CITY, SUB-BASEMENT FOUR:

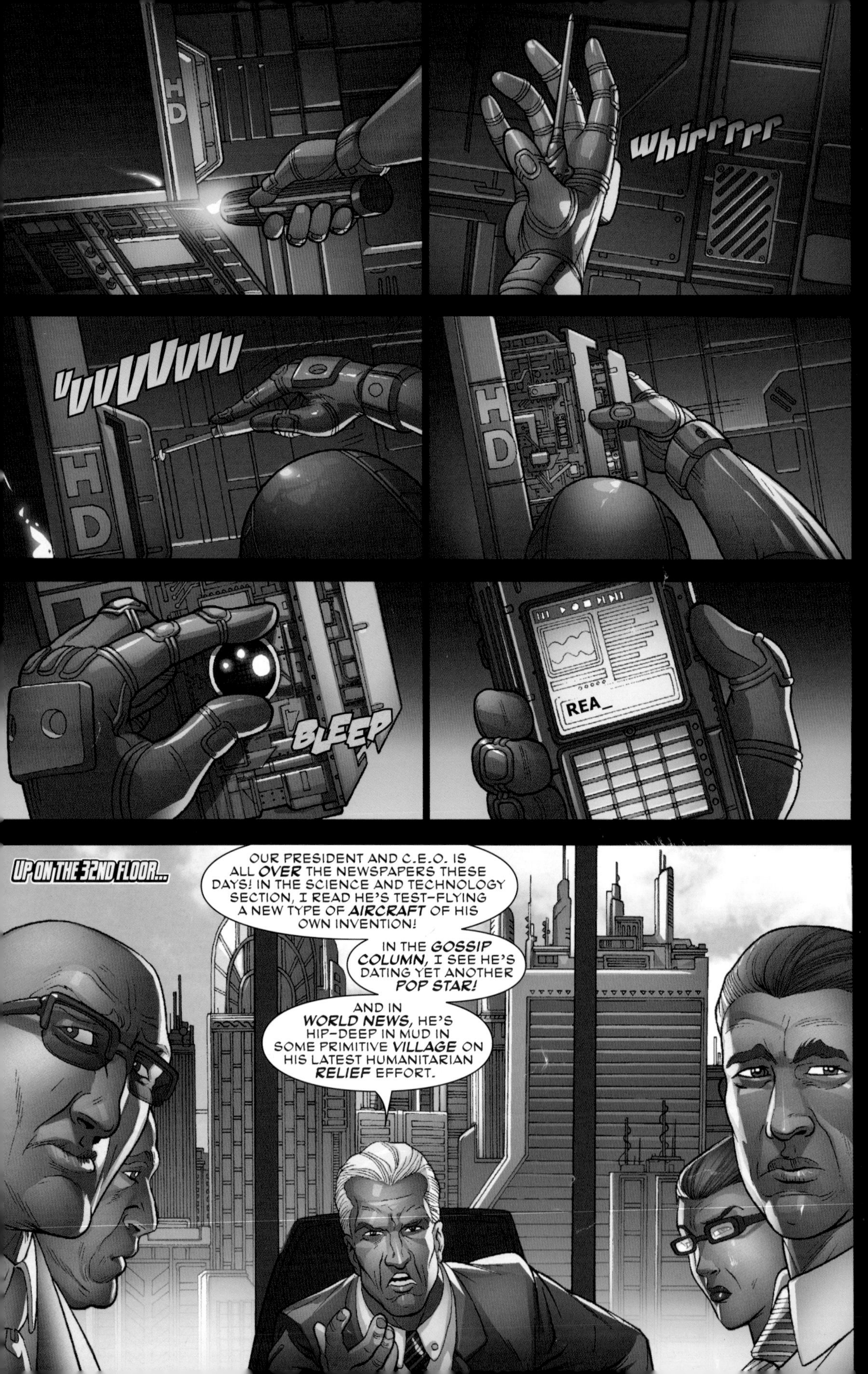
WHIRRRRR
VVVVVVVVV
BLEEP
REA_
UP ON THE 32ND FLOOR...
OUR PRESIDENT AND C.E.O. IS ALL OVER THE NEWSPAPERS THESE DAYS! IN THE SCIENCE AND TECHNOLOGY SECTION, I READ HE'S TEST-FLYING A NEW TYPE OF AIRCRAFT OF HIS OWN INVENTION!
IN THE GOSSIP COLUMN, I SEE HE'S DATING YET ANOTHER POP STAR!
AND IN WORLD NEWS, HE'S HIP-DEEP IN MUD IN SOME PRIMITIVE VILLAGE ON HIS LATEST HUMANITARIAN RELIEF EFFORT.

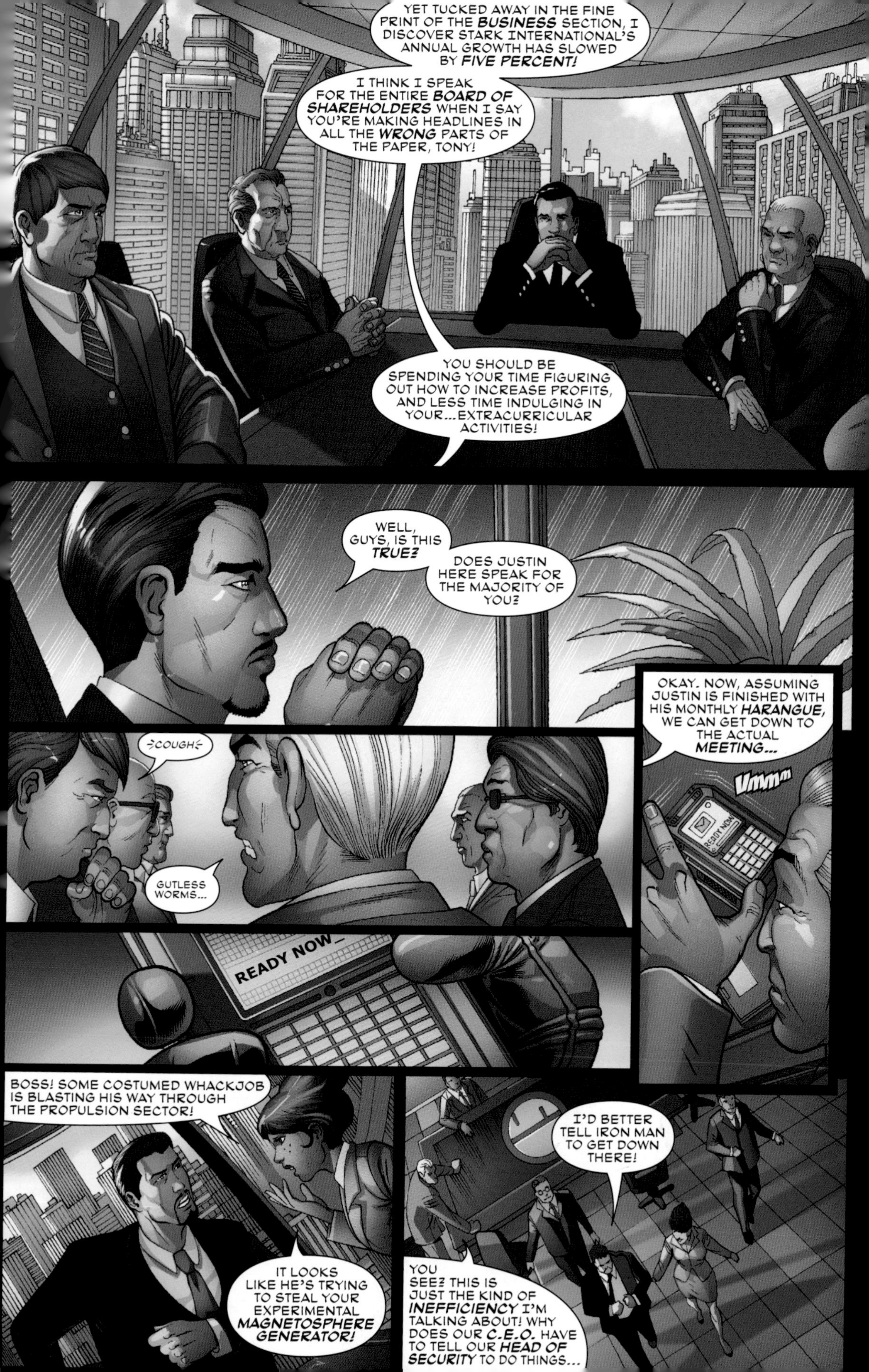
YET TUCKED AWAY IN THE FINE PRINT OF THE BUSINESS SECTION, I DISCOVER STARK INTERNATIONAL'S ANNUAL GROWTH HAS SLOWED BY FIVE PERCENT!
I THINK I SPEAK FOR THE ENTIRE BOARD OF SHAREHOLDERS WHEN I SAY YOU'RE MAKING HEADLINES IN ALL THE WRONG PARTS OF THE PAPER, TONY!
YOU SHOULD BE SPENDING YOUR TIME FIGURING OUT HOW TO INCREASE PROFITS, AND LESS TIME INDULGING IN YOUR...EXTRACURRICULAR ACTIVITIES!
WELL, GUYS, IS THIS TRUE?
DOES JUSTIN HERE SPEAK FOR THE MAJORITY OF YOU?
COUGH
GUTLESS WORMS...
OKAY. NOW, ASSUMING JUSTIN IS FINISHED WITH HIS MONTHLY HARANGUE, WE CAN GET DOWN TO THE ACTUAL MEETING...
Vmmm
READY NOW
READY NOW_
BOSS! SOME COSTUMED WHACKJOB IS BLASTING HIS WAY THROUGH THE PROPULSION SECTOR!
IT LOOKS LIKE HE'S TRYING TO STEAL YOUR EXPERIMENTAL MAGNETOSPHERE GENERATOR!
I'D BETTER TELL IRON MAN TO GET DOWN THERE!
YOU SEE? THIS IS JUST THE KIND OF INEFFICIENCY I'M TALKING ABOUT! WHY DOES OUR C.E.O. HAVE TO TELL OUR HEAD OF SECURITY TO DO THINGS...

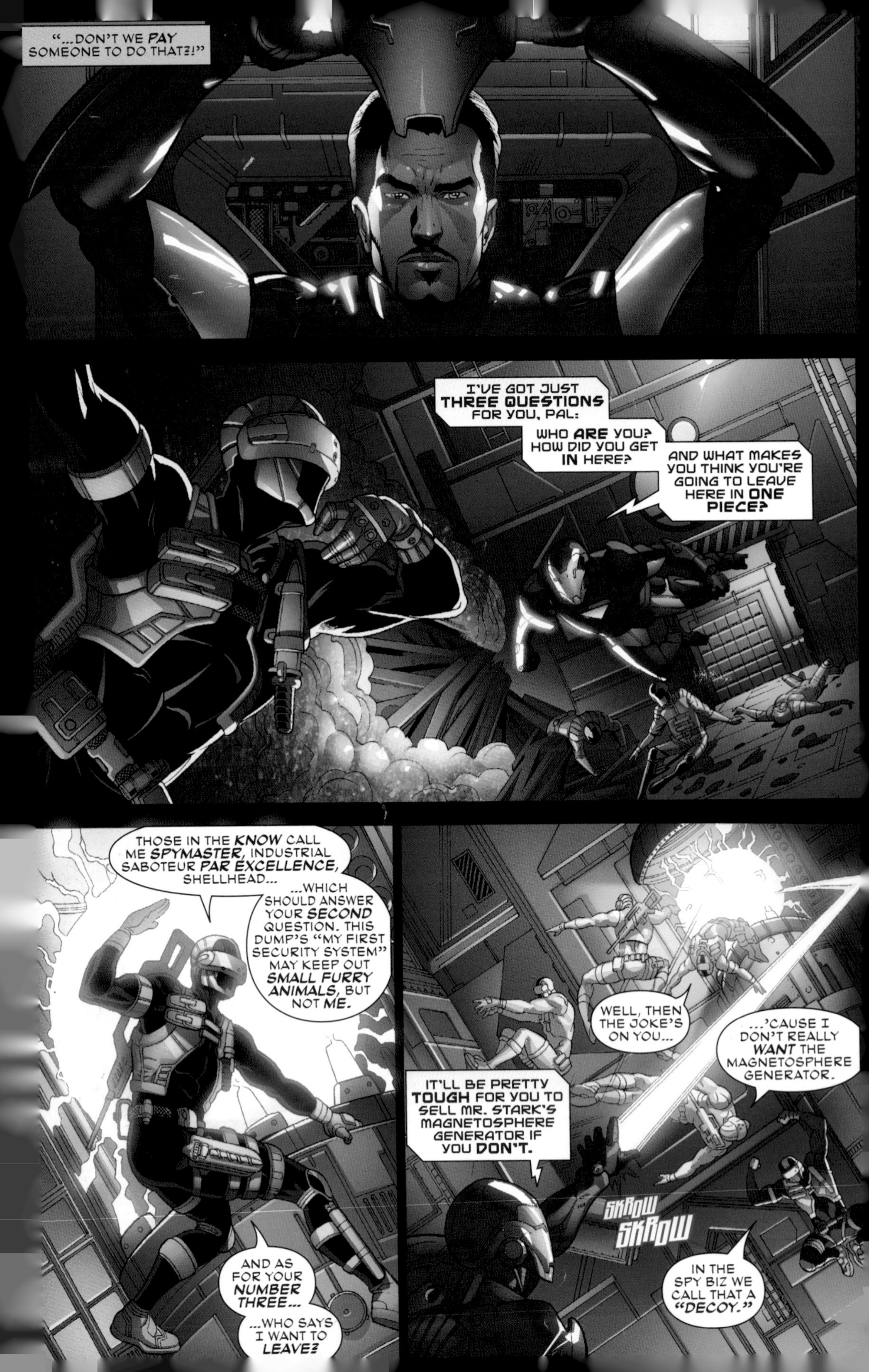
"...DON'T WE PAY SOMEONE TO DO THAT?!"
I'VE GOT JUST THREE QUESTIONS FOR YOU, PAL:
WHO ARE YOU? HOW DID YOU GET IN HERE?
AND WHAT MAKES YOU THINK YOU'RE GOING TO LEAVE HERE IN ONE PIECE?
THOSE IN THE KNOW CALL ME SPYMASTER, INDUSTRIAL SABOTEUR PAR EXCELLENCE, SHELLHEAD...
...WHICH SHOULD ANSWER YOUR SECOND QUESTION. THIS DUMP'S "MY FIRST SECURITY SYSTEM" MAY KEEP OUT SMALL FURRY ANIMALS, BUT NOT ME.
AND AS FOR YOUR NUMBER THREE...
...WHO SAYS I WANT TO LEAVE?
IT'LL BE PRETTY TOUGH FOR YOU TO SELL MR. STARK'S MAGNETOSPHERE GENERATOR IF YOU DON'T.
WELL, THEN THE JOKE'S ON YOU...
...'CAUSE I DON'T REALLY WANT THE MAGNETOSPHERE GENERATOR.
SKROW
SKROW
IN THE SPY BIZ WE CALL THAT A "DECOY."

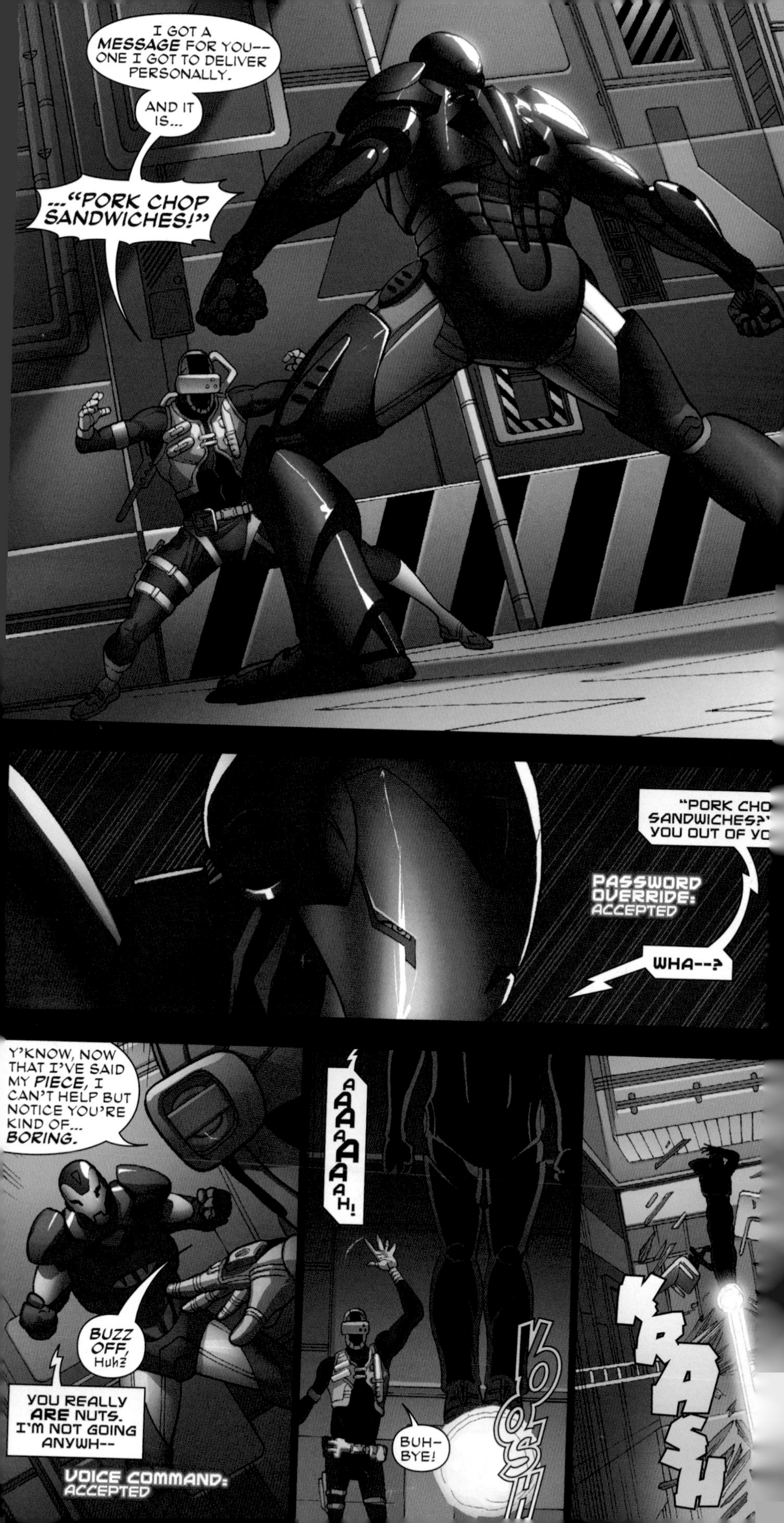
I GOT A MESSAGE FOR YOU-- ONE I GOT TO DELIVER PERSONALLY.
AND IT IS...
..."PORK CHOP SANDWICHES!"
"PORK CHO SANDWICHES?" YOU OUT OF YO
PASSWORD OVERRIDE: ACCEPTED
WHA--?
Y'KNOW, NOW THAT I'VE SAID MY PIECE, I CAN'T HELP BUT NOTICE YOU'RE KIND OF... BORING.
BUZZ OFF, Huh?
YOU REALLY ARE NUTS. I'M NOT GOING ANYWH--
VOICE COMMAND: ACCEPTED
AAAAAAAH!
BUH-BYE!
WOOSH
KRASH

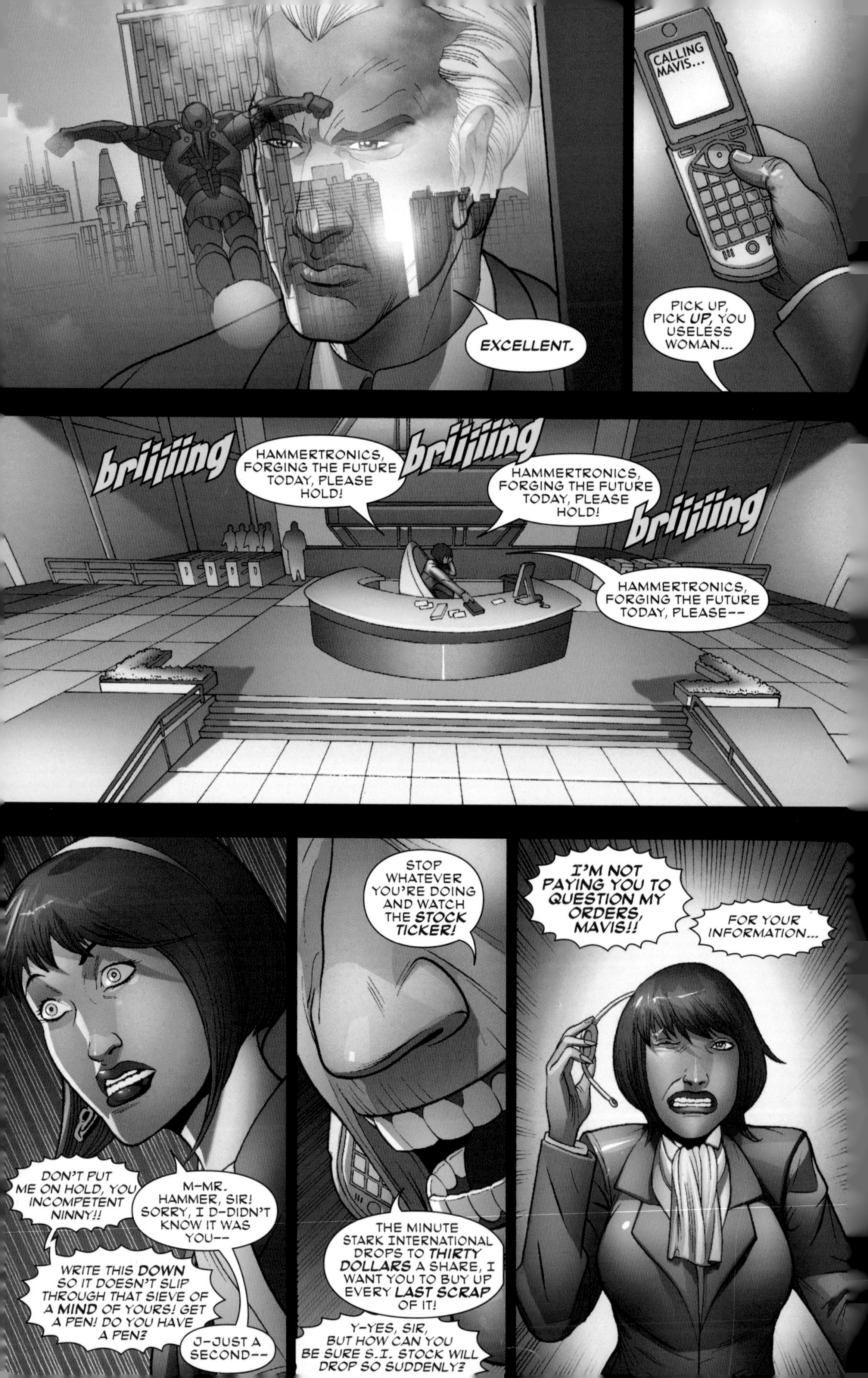
CALLING MAVIS...
EXCELLENT.
PICK UP, PICK UP, YOU USELESS WOMAN...
briiiiing
HAMMERTRONICS, FORGING THE FUTURE TODAY, PLEASE HOLD!
briiiiing
HAMMERTRONICS, FORGING THE FUTURE TODAY, PLEASE HOLD!
briiiiing
HAMMERTRONICS, FORGING THE FUTURE TODAY, PLEASE--
DON'T PUT ME ON HOLD, YOU INCOMPETENT NINNY!!
M-MR. HAMMER, SIR! SORRY, I D-DIDN'T KNOW IT WAS YOU--
WRITE THIS DOWN SO IT DOESN'T SLIP THROUGH THAT SIEVE OF A MIND OF YOURS! GET A PEN! DO YOU HAVE A PEN?
J-JUST A SECOND--
STOP WHATEVER YOU'RE DOING AND WATCH THE STOCK TICKER!
THE MINUTE STARK INTERNATIONAL DROPS TO THIRTY DOLLARS A SHARE, I WANT YOU TO BUY UP EVERY LAST SCRAP OF IT!
Y-YES, SIR, BUT HOW CAN YOU BE SURE S.I. STOCK WILL DROP SO SUDDENLY?
I'M NOT PAYING YOU TO QUESTION MY ORDERS, MAVIS!!
FOR YOUR INFORMATION...

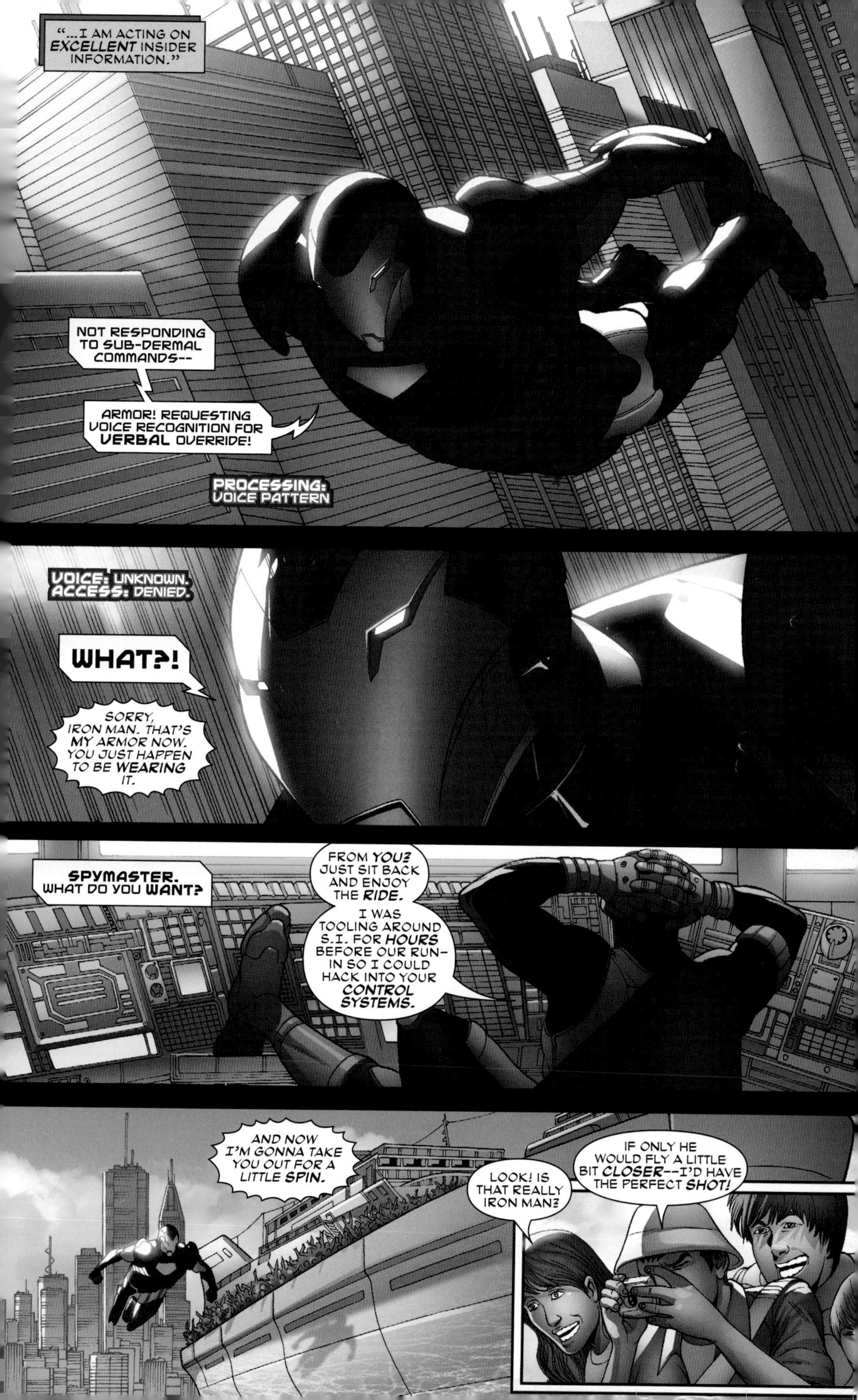
"...I AM ACTING ON EXCELLENT INSIDER INFORMATION."
NOT RESPONDING TO SUB-DERMAL COMMANDS--
ARMOR! REQUESTING VOICE RECOGNITION FOR VERBAL OVERRIDE!
PROCESSING: VOICE PATTERN
VOICE: UNKNOWN. ACCESS: DENIED.
WHAT?!
SORRY, IRON MAN. THAT'S MY ARMOR NOW. YOU JUST HAPPEN TO BE WEARING IT.
SPYMASTER. WHAT DO YOU WANT?
FROM YOU? JUST SIT BACK AND ENJOY THE RIDE.
I WAS TOOLING AROUND S.I. FOR HOURS BEFORE OUR RUN-IN SO I COULD HACK INTO YOUR CONTROL SYSTEMS.
AND NOW I'M GONNA TAKE YOU OUT FOR A LITTLE SPIN.
LOOK! IS THAT REALLY IRON MAN?
IF ONLY HE WOULD FLY A LITTLE BIT CLOSER--I'D HAVE THE PERFECT SHOT!

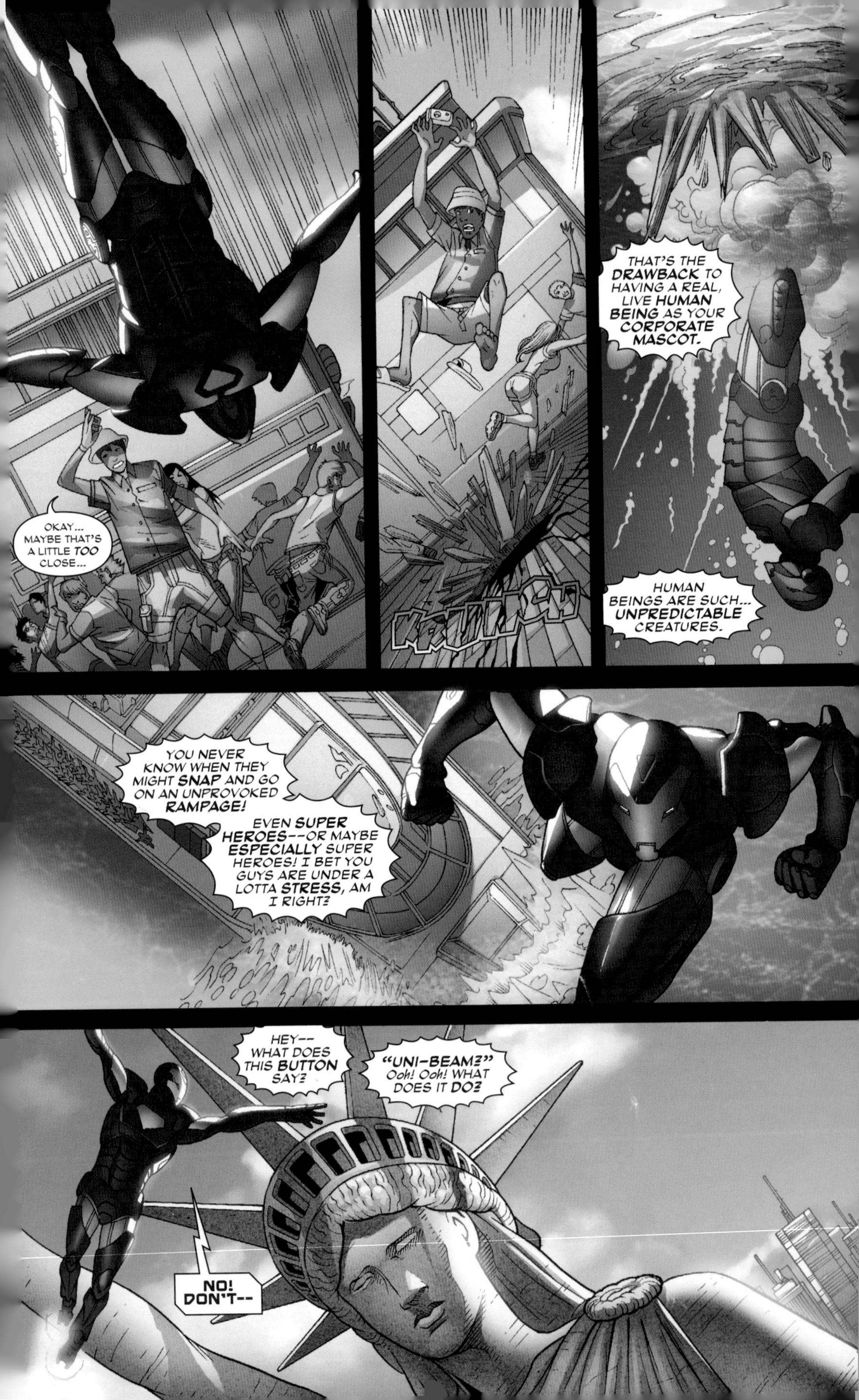
OKAY... MAYBE THAT'S A LITTLE TOO CLOSE...
THAT'S THE DRAWBACK TO HAVING A REAL, LIVE HUMAN BEING AS YOUR CORPORATE MASCOT.
HUMAN BEINGS ARE SUCH... UNPREDICTABLE CREATURES.
YOU NEVER KNOW WHEN THEY MIGHT SNAP AND GO ON AN UNPROVOKED RAMPAGE!
EVEN SUPER HEROES--OR MAYBE ESPECIALLY SUPER HEROES! I BET YOU GUYS ARE UNDER A LOTTA STRESS, AM I RIGHT?
HEY-- WHAT DOES THIS BUTTON SAY?
"UNI-BEAM?" Ooh! Ooh! WHAT DOES IT DO?
NO! DON'T--

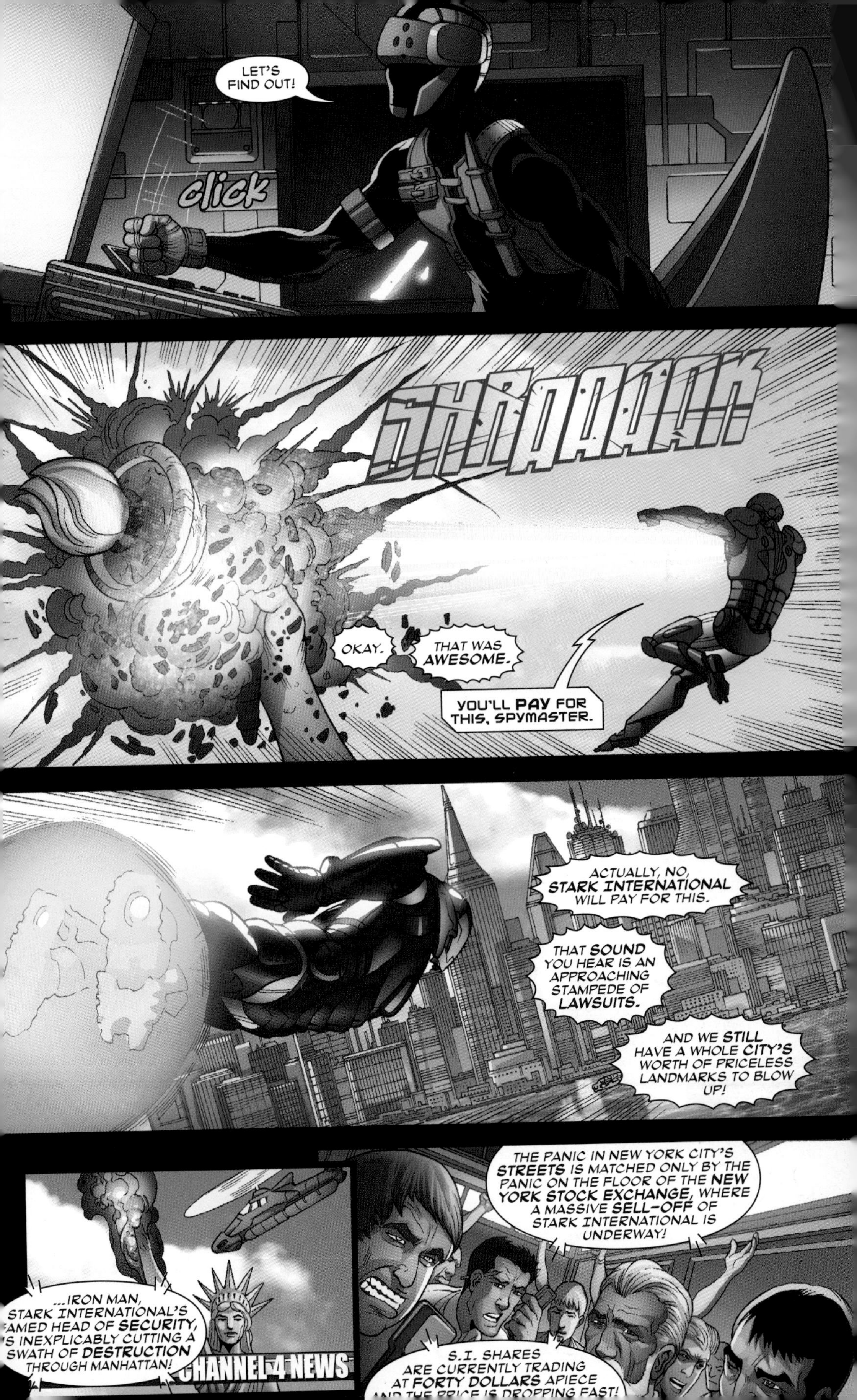
LET'S FIND OUT!
click
OKAY.
THAT WAS AWESOME.
YOU'LL PAY FOR THIS, SPYMASTER.
ACTUALLY, NO, STARK INTERNATIONAL WILL PAY FOR THIS.
THAT SOUND YOU HEAR IS AN APPROACHING STAMPEDE OF LAWSUITS.
AND WE STILL HAVE A WHOLE CITY'S WORTH OF PRICELESS LANDMARKS TO BLOW UP!
...IRON MAN, STARK INTERNATIONAL'S AMED HEAD OF SECURITY, S INEXPLICABLY CUTTING A SWATH OF DESTRUCTION THROUGH MANHATTAN!
CHANNEL 4 NEWS
THE PANIC IN NEW YORK CITY'S STREETS IS MATCHED ONLY BY THE PANIC ON THE FLOOR OF THE NEW YORK STOCK EXCHANGE, WHERE A MASSIVE SELL-OFF OF STARK INTERNATIONAL IS UNDERWAY!
S.I. SHARES ARE CURRENTLY TRADING AT FORTY DOLLARS APIECE

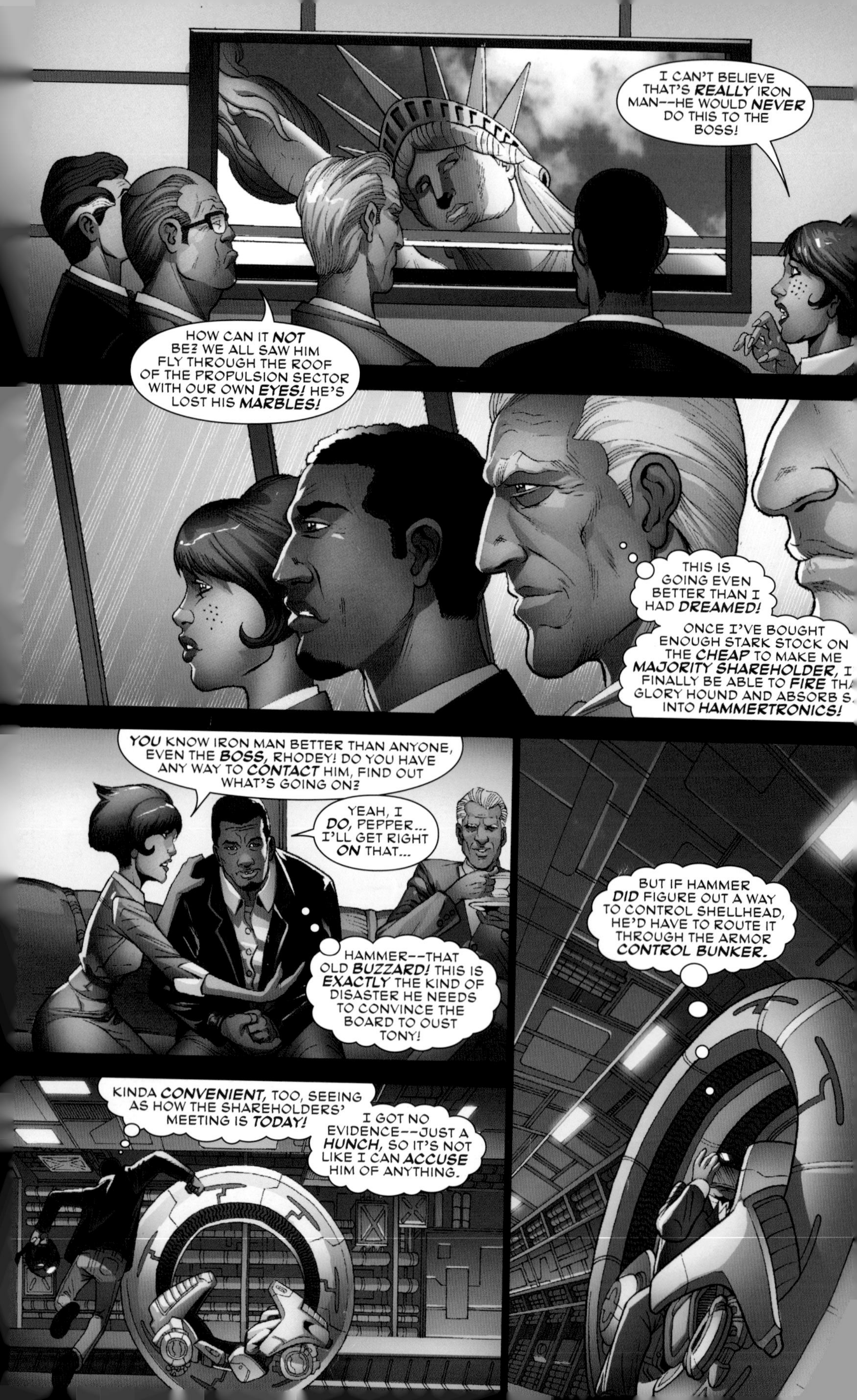
I CAN'T BELIEVE THAT'S REALLY IRON MAN--HE WOULD NEVER DO THIS TO THE BOSS!
HOW CAN IT NOT BE? WE ALL SAW HIM FLY THROUGH THE ROOF OF THE PROPULSION SECTOR WITH OUR OWN EYES! HE'S LOST HIS MARBLES!
THIS IS GOING EVEN BETTER THAN I HAD DREAMED!
ONCE I'VE BOUGHT ENOUGH STARK STOCK ON THE CHEAP TO MAKE ME MAJORITY SHAREHOLDER, I FINALLY BE ABLE TO FIRE THA GLORY HOUND AND ABSORB S. INTO HAMMERTRONICS!
YOU KNOW IRON MAN BETTER THAN ANYONE, EVEN THE BOSS, RHODEY! DO YOU HAVE ANY WAY TO CONTACT HIM, FIND OUT WHAT'S GOING ON?
YEAH, I DO, PEPPER... I'LL GET RIGHT ON THAT...
HAMMER--THAT OLD BUZZARD! THIS IS EXACTLY THE KIND OF DISASTER HE NEEDS TO CONVINCE THE BOARD TO OUST TONY!
BUT IF HAMMER DID FIGURE OUT A WAY TO CONTROL SHELLHEAD, HE'D HAVE TO ROUTE IT THROUGH THE ARMOR CONTROL BUNKER.
KINDA CONVENIENT, TOO, SEEING AS HOW THE SHAREHOLDERS' MEETING IS TODAY!
I GOT NO EVIDENCE--JUST A HUNCH, SO IT'S NOT LIKE I CAN ACCUSE HIM OF ANYTHING.

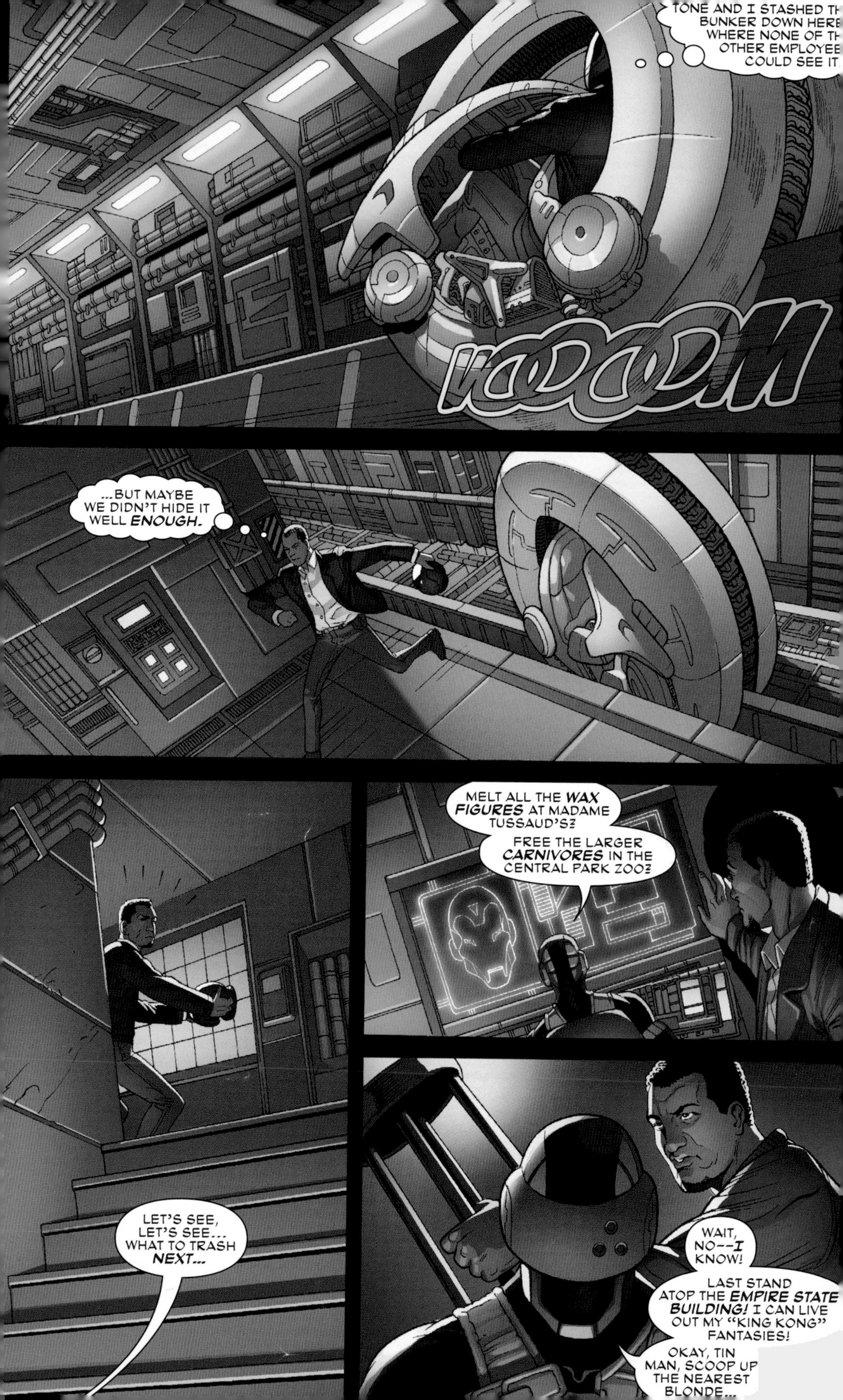
TONE AND I STASHED TH
BUNKER DOWN HERE
WHERE NONE OF TH
OTHER EMPLOYEE
COULD SEE IT.
VROOOM
...BUT MAYBE WE DIDN'T HIDE IT WELL *ENOUGH.*
LET'S SEE, LET'S SEE... WHAT TO TRASH *NEXT...*
MELT ALL THE *WAX FIGURES* AT MADAME TUSSAUD'S?
FREE THE LARGER *CARNIVORES* IN THE CENTRAL PARK ZOO?
WAIT, NO--*I* KNOW!
LAST STAND ATOP THE *EMPIRE STATE BUILDING!* I CAN LIVE OUT MY "KING KONG" FANTASIES!
OKAY, TIN MAN, SCOOP UP THE NEAREST BLONDE...

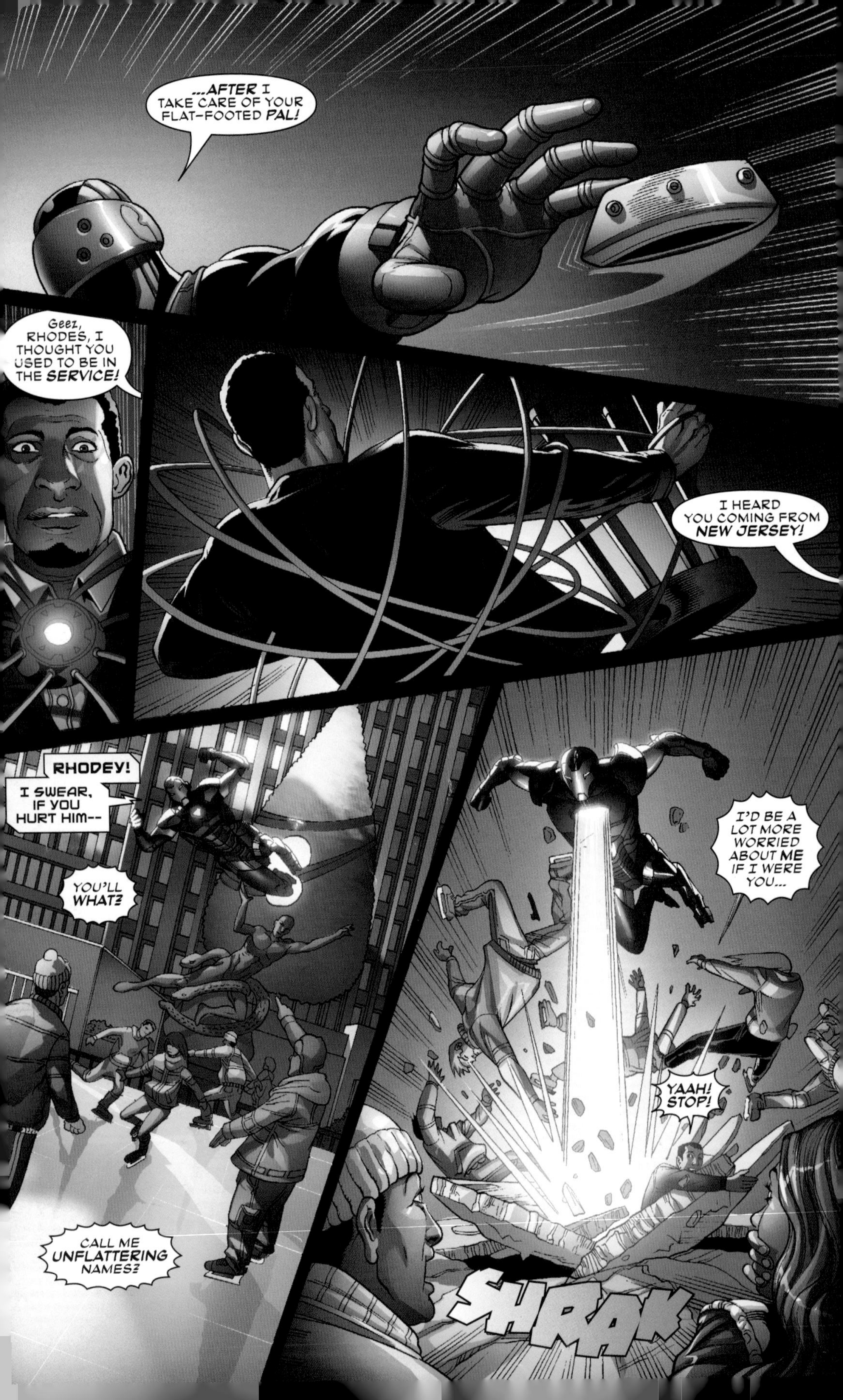
...AFTER I TAKE CARE OF YOUR FLAT-FOOTED PAL!
Geez, RHODES, I THOUGHT YOU USED TO BE IN THE SERVICE!
I HEARD YOU COMING FROM NEW JERSEY!
RHODEY!
I SWEAR, IF YOU HURT HIM--
YOU'LL WHAT?
CALL ME UNFLATTERING NAMES?
I'D BE A LOT MORE WORRIED ABOUT ME IF I WERE YOU...
YAAH! STOP!
SHRAK

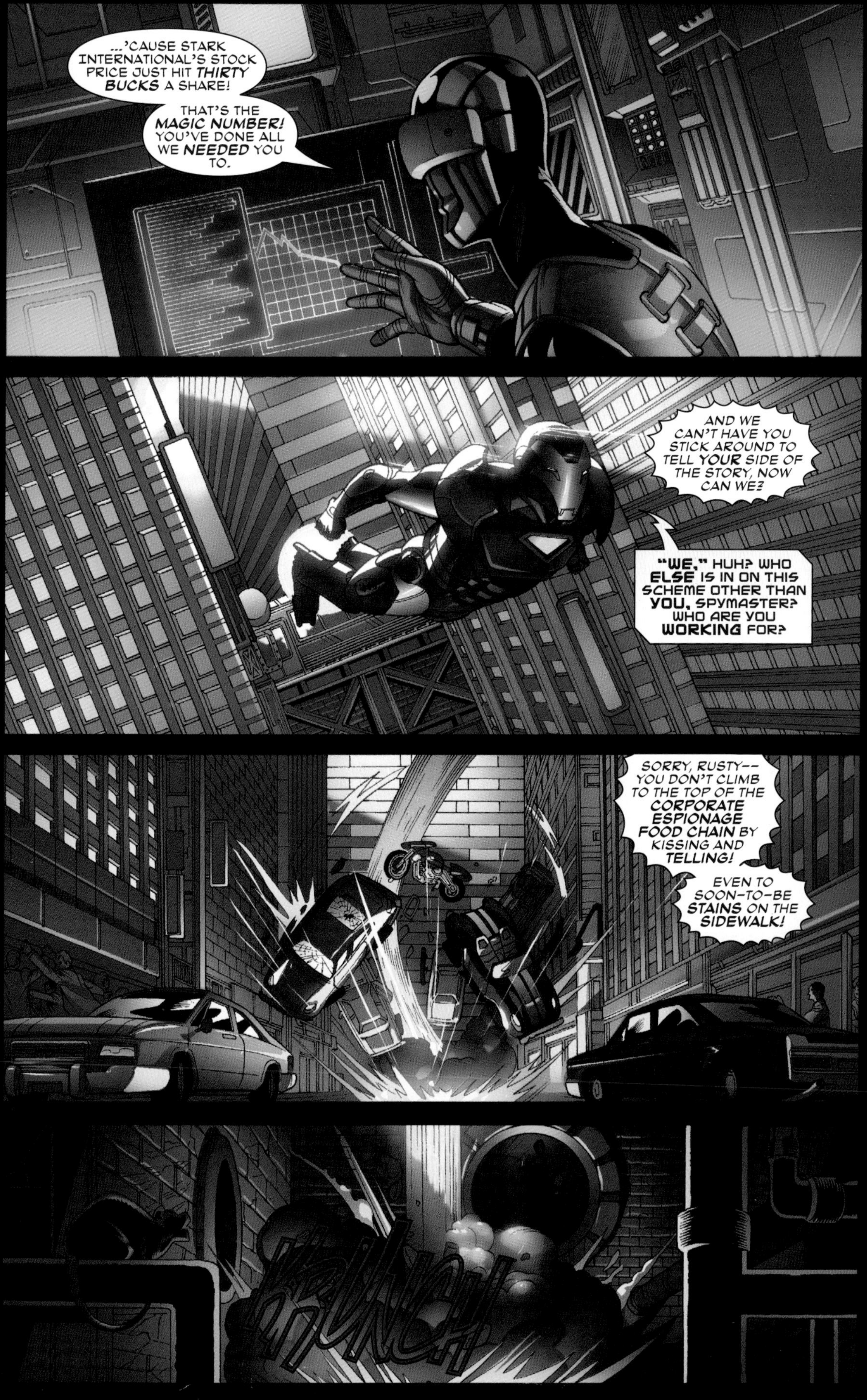
...'CAUSE STARK INTERNATIONAL'S STOCK PRICE JUST HIT THIRTY BUCKS A SHARE!
THAT'S THE MAGIC NUMBER! YOU'VE DONE ALL WE NEEDED YOU TO.
AND WE CAN'T HAVE YOU STICK AROUND TO TELL YOUR SIDE OF THE STORY, NOW CAN WE?
"WE," HUH? WHO ELSE IS IN ON THIS SCHEME OTHER THAN YOU, SPYMASTER? WHO ARE YOU WORKING FOR?
SORRY, RUSTY-- YOU DON'T CLIMB TO THE TOP OF THE CORPORATE ESPIONAGE FOOD CHAIN BY KISSING AND TELLING!
EVEN TO SOON-TO-BE STAINS ON THE SIDEWALK!
KRUNCH

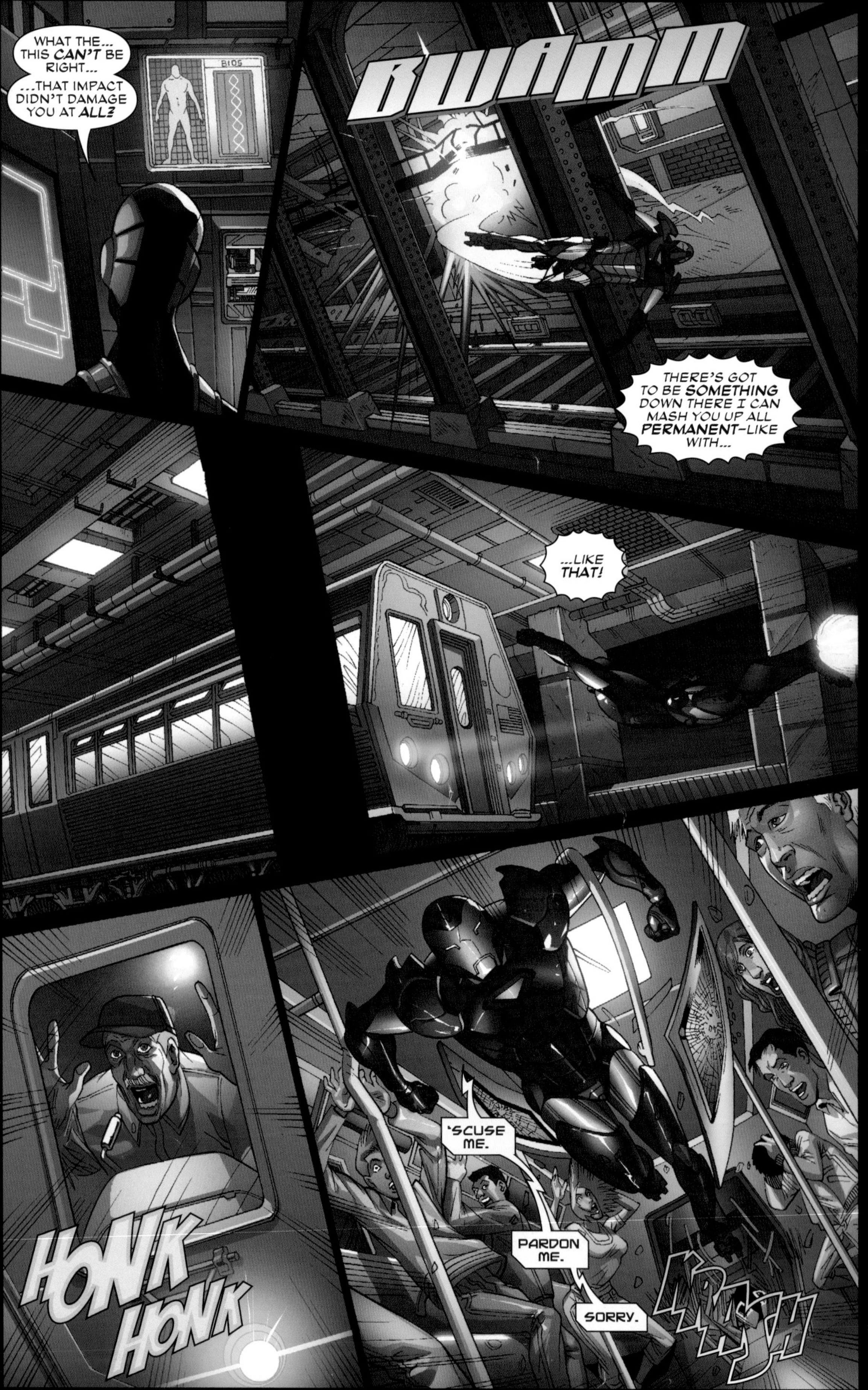
WHAT THE... THIS CAN'T BE RIGHT... ...THAT IMPACT DIDN'T DAMAGE YOU AT ALL?
BIOS
BWAMM
THERE'S GOT TO BE SOMETHING DOWN THERE I CAN MASH YOU UP ALL PERMANENT-LIKE WITH...
...LIKE THAT!
HONK HONK
'SCUSE ME.
PARDON ME.
SORRY.

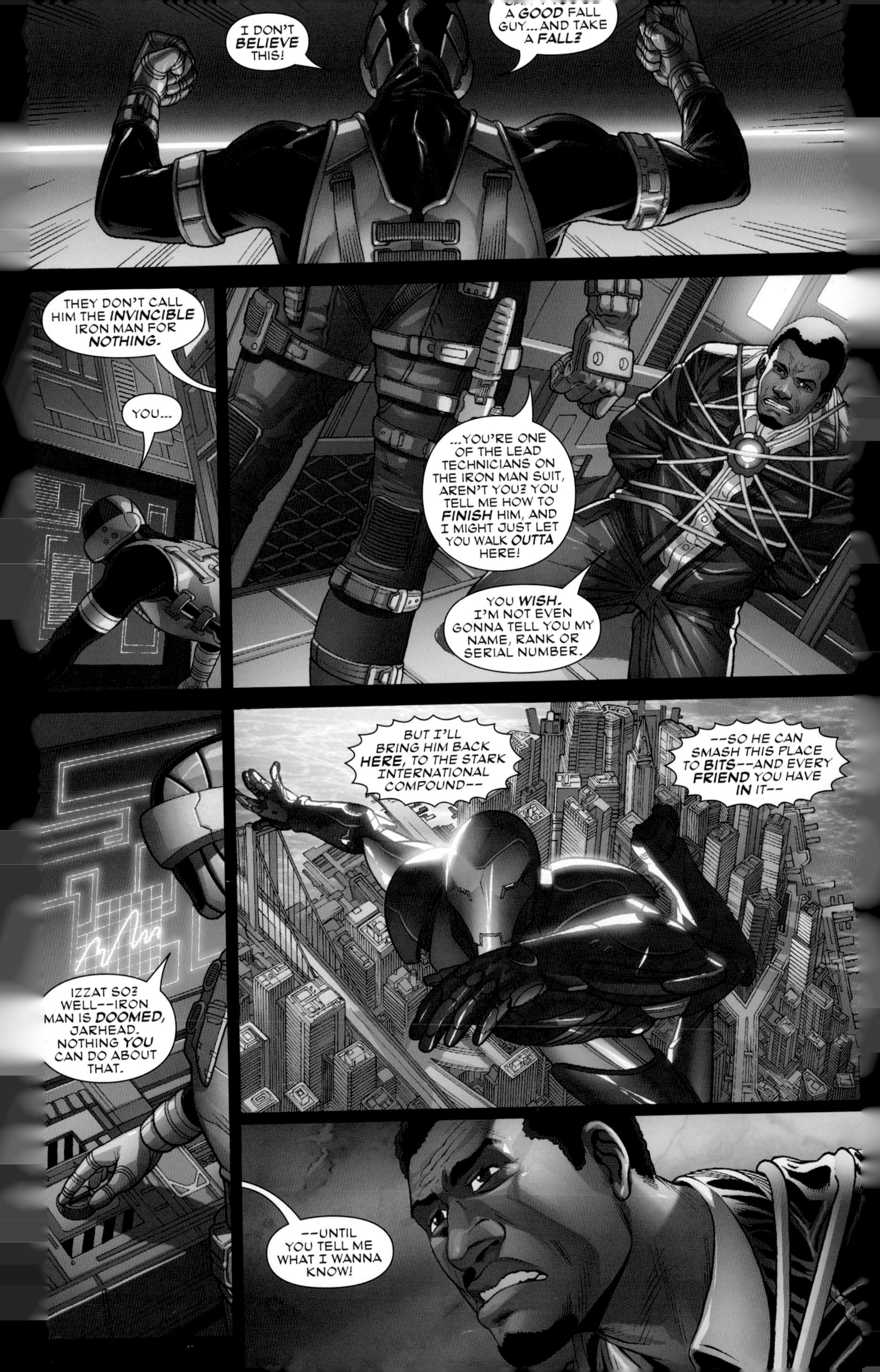

I DON'T BELIEVE THIS!
A GOOD FALL GUY...AND TAKE A FALL?
THEY DON'T CALL HIM THE INVINCIBLE IRON MAN FOR NOTHING.
YOU...
...YOU'RE ONE OF THE LEAD TECHNICIANS ON THE IRON MAN SUIT, AREN'T YOU? YOU TELL ME HOW TO FINISH HIM, AND I MIGHT JUST LET YOU WALK OUTTA HERE!
YOU WISH. I'M NOT EVEN GONNA TELL YOU MY NAME, RANK OR SERIAL NUMBER.
IZZAT SO? WELL--IRON MAN IS DOOMED, JARHEAD. NOTHING YOU CAN DO ABOUT THAT.
BUT I'LL BRING HIM BACK HERE, TO THE STARK INTERNATIONAL COMPOUND--
--SO HE CAN SMASH THIS PLACE TO BITS--AND EVERY FRIEND YOU HAVE IN IT--
--UNTIL YOU TELL ME WHAT I WANNA KNOW!

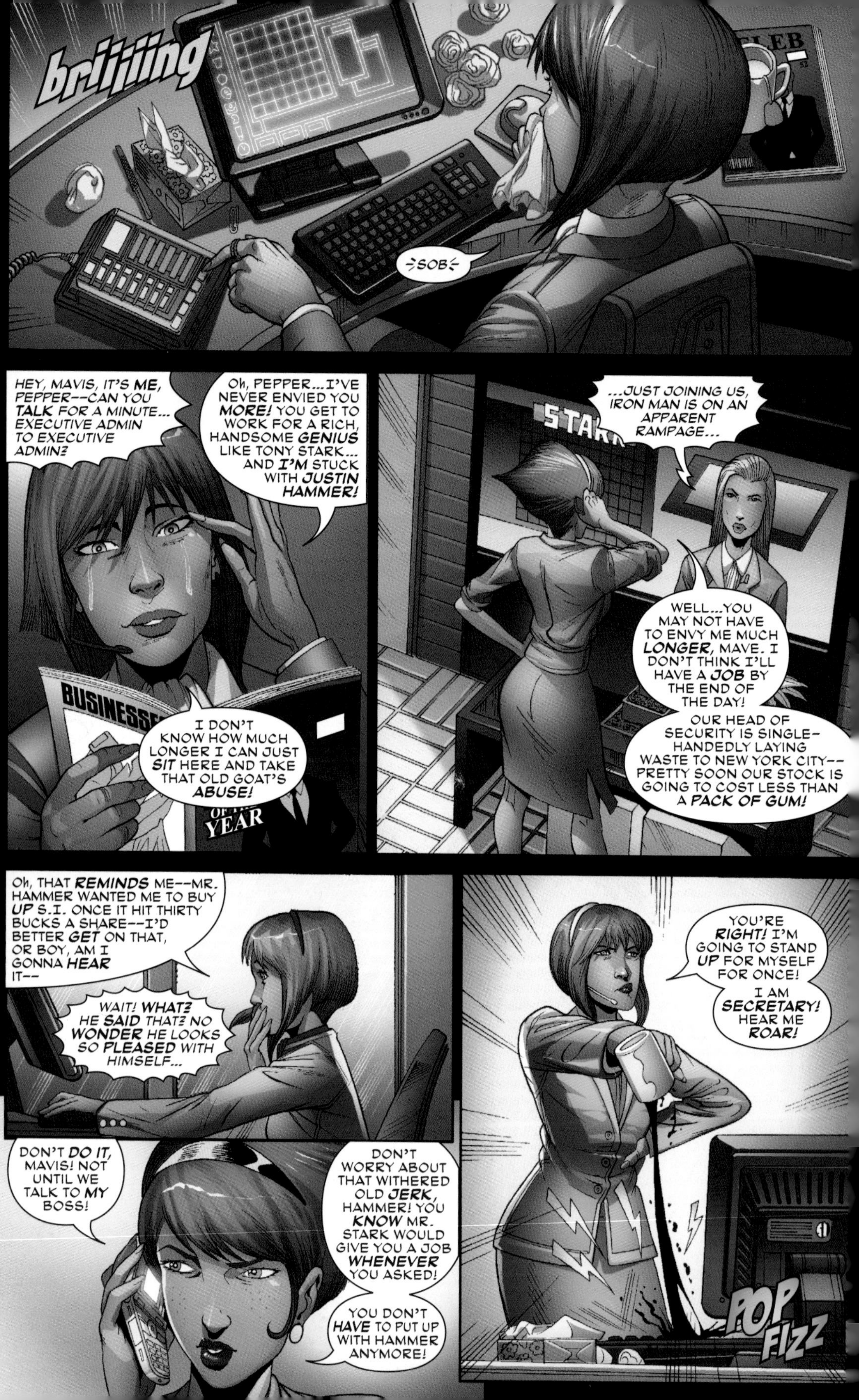
brijiiing
SOB
HEY, MAVIS, IT'S ME, PEPPER--CAN YOU TALK FOR A MINUTE... EXECUTIVE ADMIN TO EXECUTIVE ADMIN?
Oh, PEPPER...I'VE NEVER ENVIED YOU MORE! YOU GET TO WORK FOR A RICH, HANDSOME GENIUS LIKE TONY STARK... AND I'M STUCK WITH JUSTIN HAMMER!
BUSINESS
OF THE YEAR
I DON'T KNOW HOW MUCH LONGER I CAN JUST SIT HERE AND TAKE THAT OLD GOAT'S ABUSE!
STARK
...JUST JOINING US, IRON MAN IS ON AN APPARENT RAMPAGE...
WELL...YOU MAY NOT HAVE TO ENVY ME MUCH LONGER, MAVE. I DON'T THINK I'LL HAVE A JOB BY THE END OF THE DAY!
OUR HEAD OF SECURITY IS SINGLE-HANDEDLY LAYING WASTE TO NEW YORK CITY--PRETTY SOON OUR STOCK IS GOING TO COST LESS THAN A PACK OF GUM!
Oh, THAT REMINDS ME--MR. HAMMER WANTED ME TO BUY UP S.I. ONCE IT HIT THIRTY BUCKS A SHARE--I'D BETTER GET ON THAT, OR BOY, AM I GONNA HEAR IT--
WAIT! WHAT? HE SAID THAT? NO WONDER HE LOOKS SO PLEASED WITH HIMSELF...
DON'T DO IT, MAVIS! NOT UNTIL WE TALK TO MY BOSS!
DON'T WORRY ABOUT THAT WITHERED OLD JERK, HAMMER! YOU KNOW MR. STARK WOULD GIVE YOU A JOB WHENEVER YOU ASKED!
YOU DON'T HAVE TO PUT UP WITH HAMMER ANYMORE!
YOU'RE RIGHT! I'M GOING TO STAND UP FOR MYSELF FOR ONCE!
I AM SECRETARY! HEAR ME ROAR!
POP
FIZZ

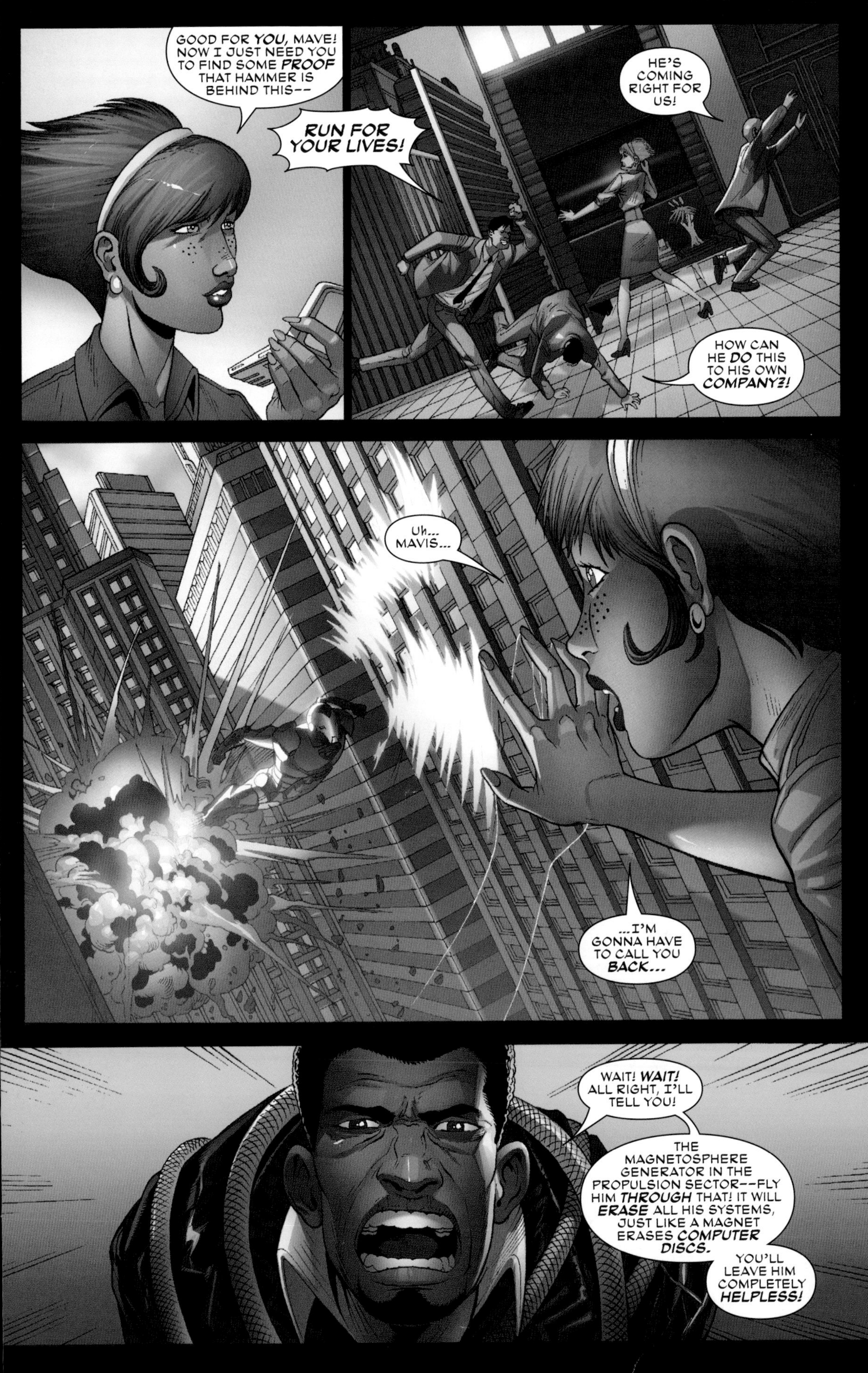
GOOD FOR YOU, MAVE! NOW I JUST NEED YOU TO FIND SOME PROOF THAT HAMMER IS BEHIND THIS--
RUN FOR YOUR LIVES!
HE'S COMING RIGHT FOR US!
HOW CAN HE DO THIS TO HIS OWN COMPANY?!
Uh... MAVIS...
...I'M GONNA HAVE TO CALL YOU BACK...
WAIT! WAIT! ALL RIGHT, I'LL TELL YOU!
THE MAGNETOSPHERE GENERATOR IN THE PROPULSION SECTOR--FLY HIM THROUGH THAT! IT WILL ERASE ALL HIS SYSTEMS, JUST LIKE A MAGNET ERASES COMPUTER DISCS.
YOU'LL LEAVE HIM COMPLETELY HELPLESS!

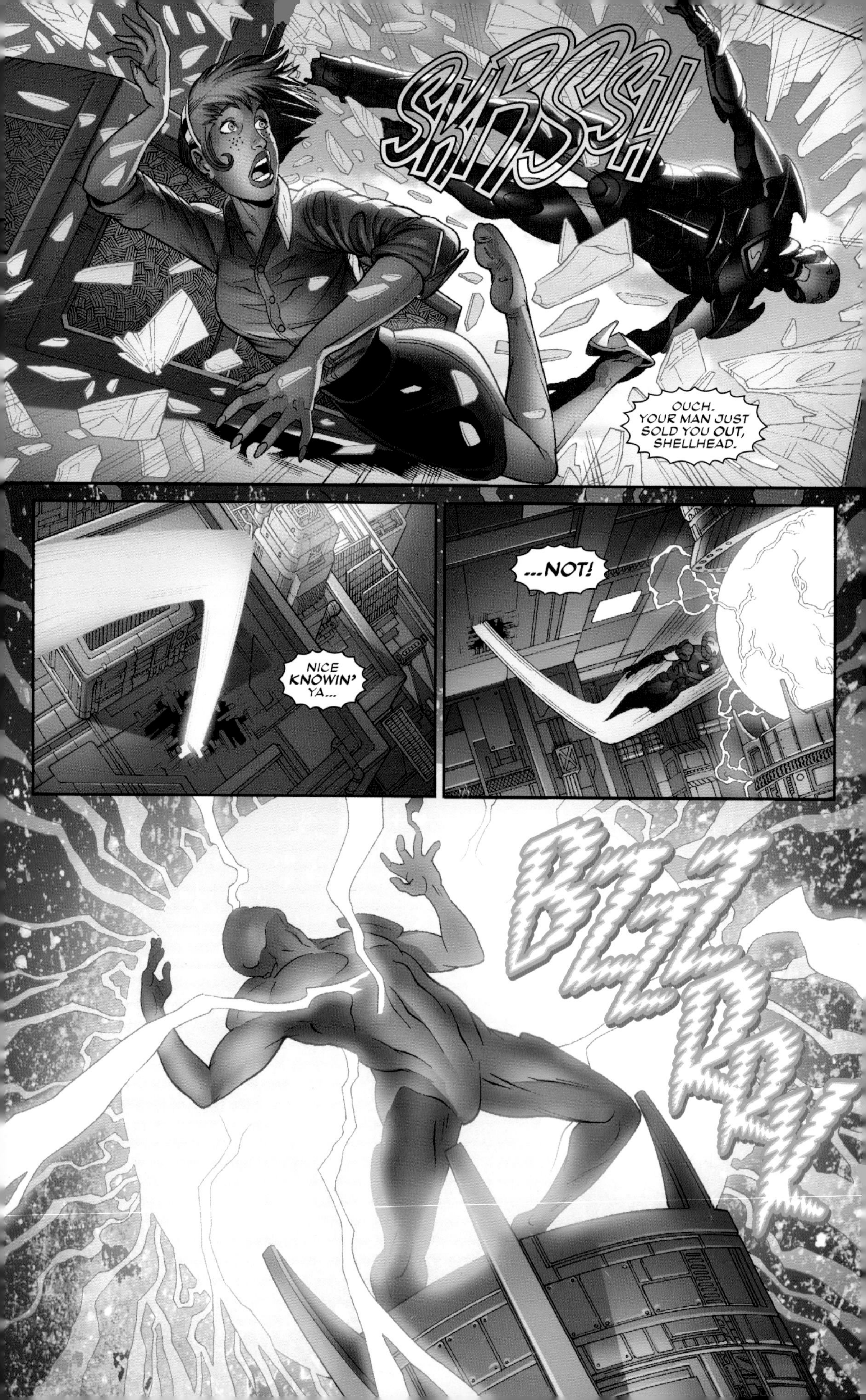
SKRSSH
OUCH. YOUR MAN JUST SOLD YOU OUT, SHELLHEAD.
NICE KNOWIN' YA...
...NOT!
BZZRAK!

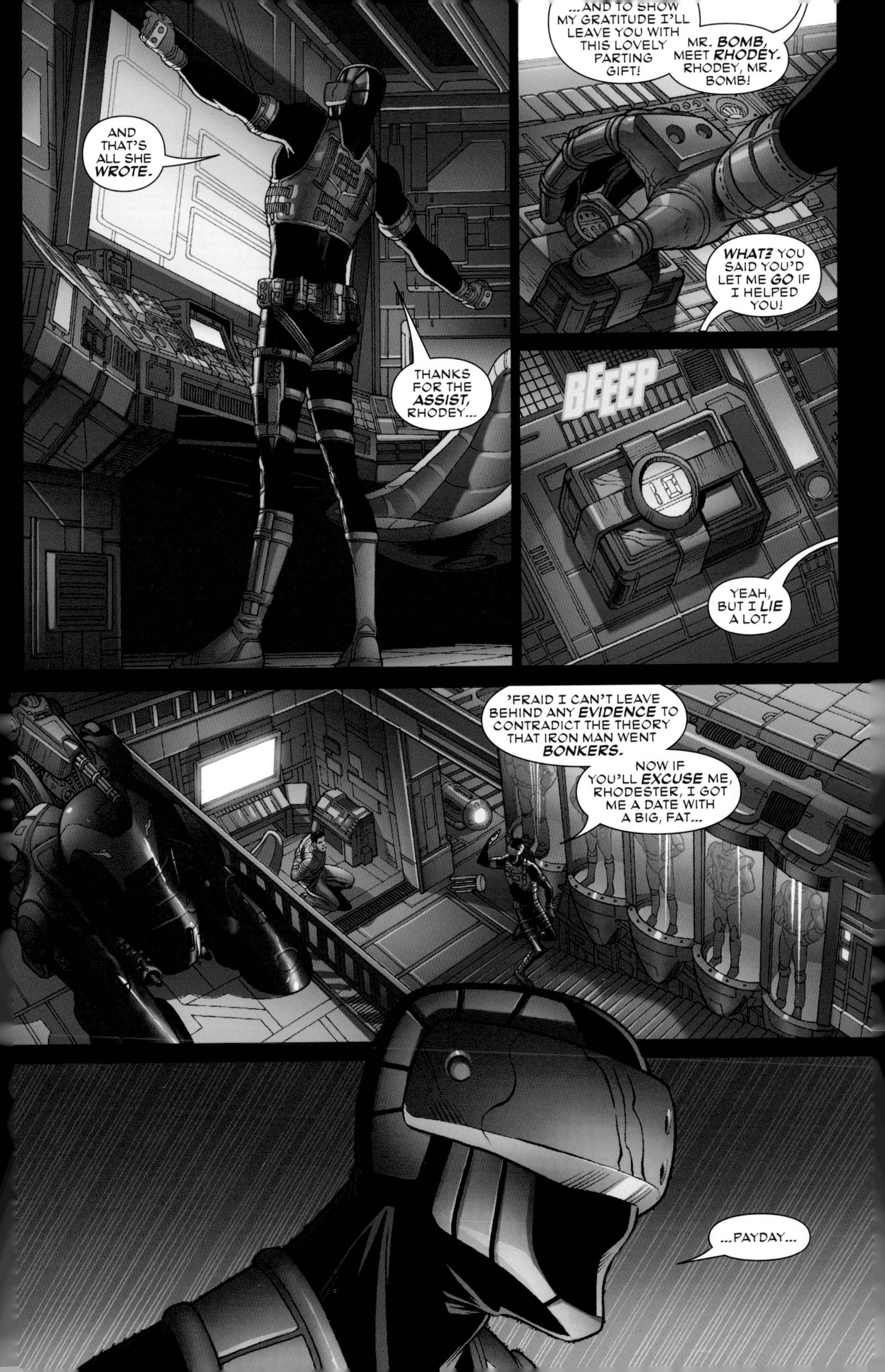
AND THAT'S ALL SHE WROTE.
THANKS FOR THE ASSIST, RHODEY...
...AND TO SHOW MY GRATITUDE I'LL LEAVE YOU WITH THIS LOVELY PARTING GIFT!
MR. BOMB, MEET RHODEY. RHODEY, MR. BOMB!
WHAT? YOU SAID YOU'D LET ME GO IF I HELPED YOU!
BEEEP
YEAH, BUT I LIE A LOT.
'FRAID I CAN'T LEAVE BEHIND ANY EVIDENCE TO CONTRADICT THE THEORY THAT IRON MAN WENT BONKERS.
NOW IF YOU'LL EXCUSE ME, RHODESTER, I GOT ME A DATE WITH A BIG, FAT...
...PAYDAY...

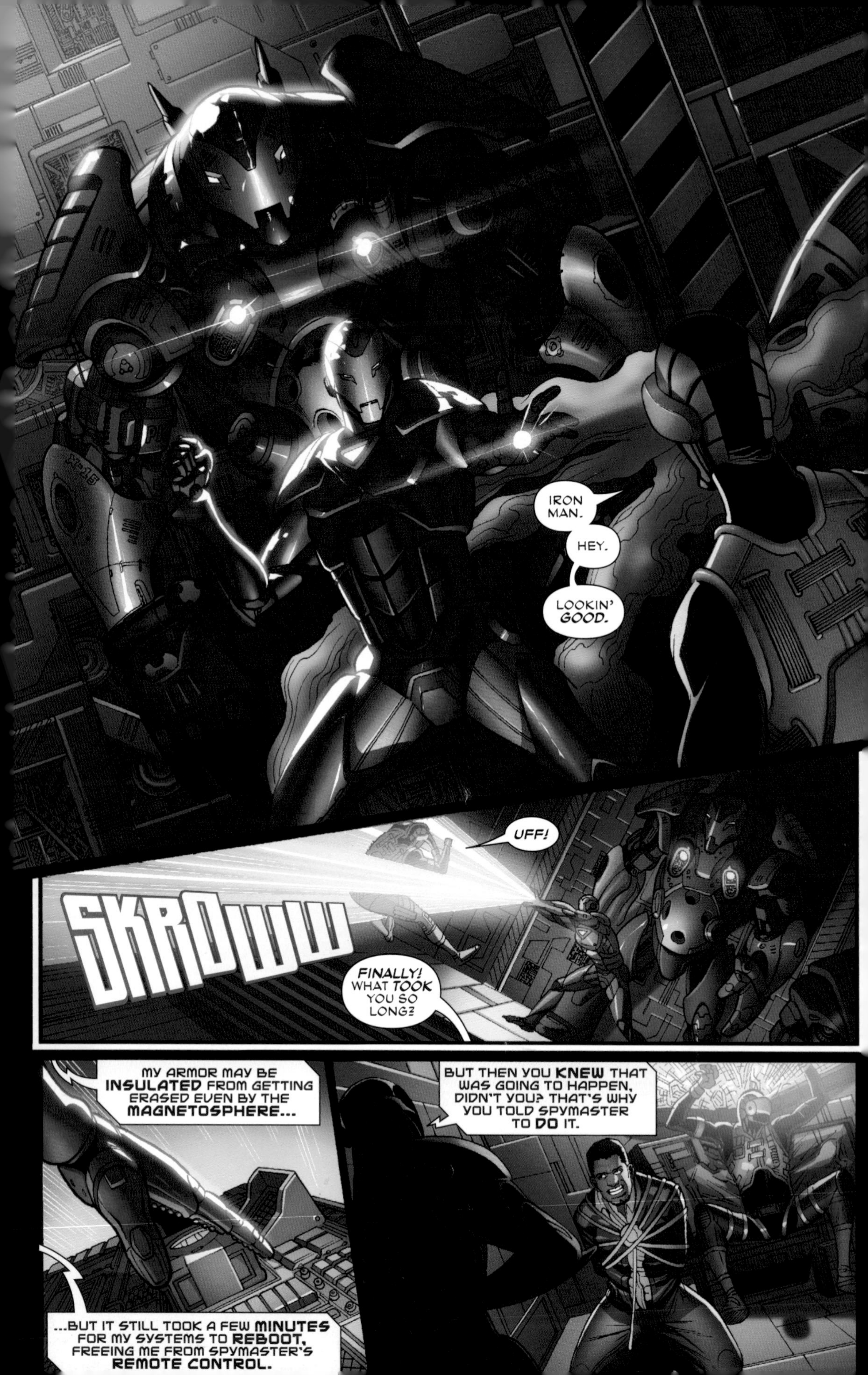
IRON MAN.
HEY.
LOOKIN' GOOD.
UFF!
SKROWW
FINALLY! WHAT TOOK YOU SO LONG?
MY ARMOR MAY BE INSULATED FROM GETTING ERASED EVEN BY THE MAGNETOSPHERE...
...BUT IT STILL TOOK A FEW MINUTES FOR MY SYSTEMS TO REBOOT, FREEING ME FROM SPYMASTER'S REMOTE CONTROL.
BUT THEN YOU KNEW THAT WAS GOING TO HAPPEN, DIDN'T YOU? THAT'S WHY YOU TOLD SPYMASTER TO DO IT.

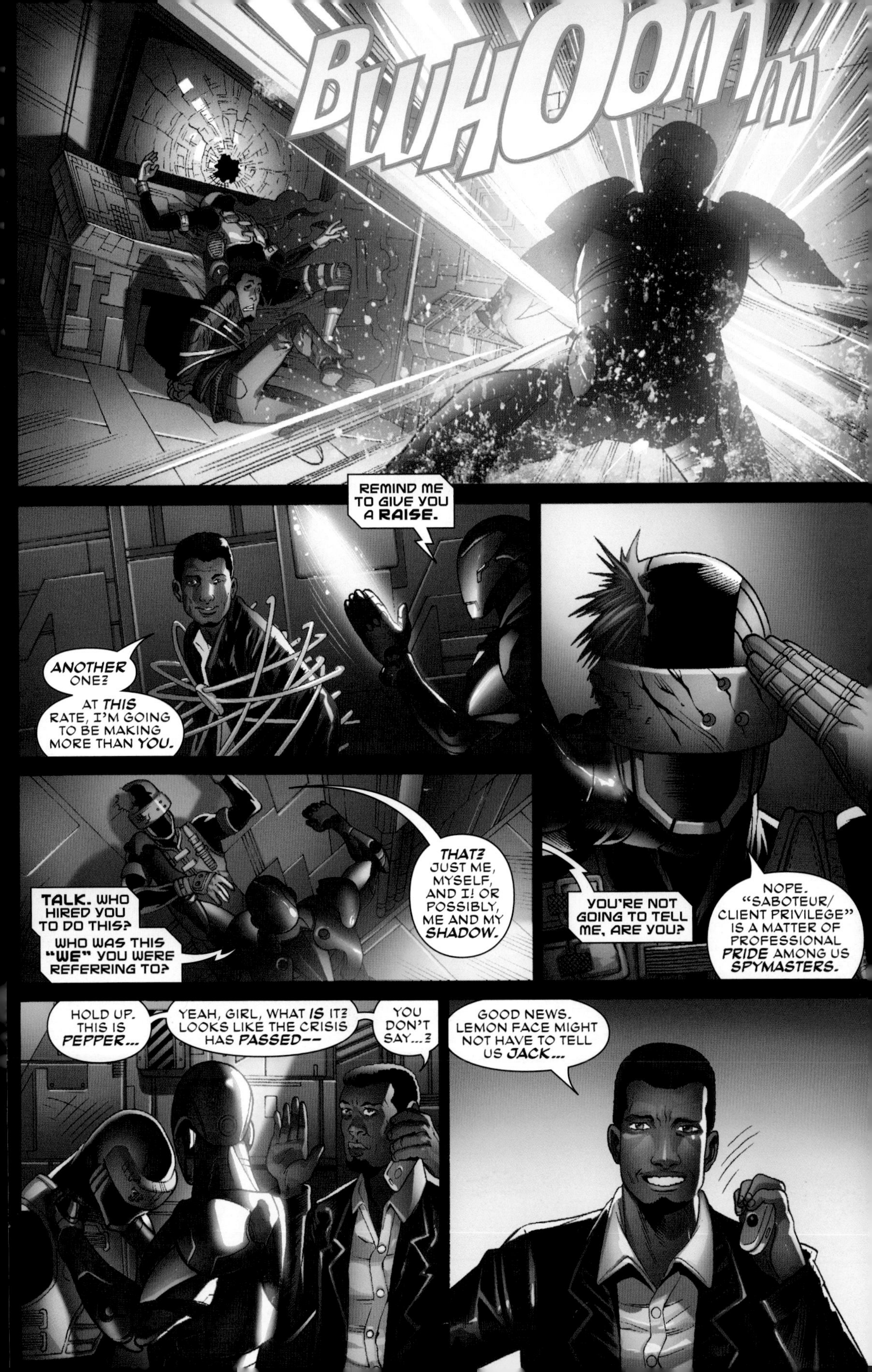
BWHOOM
REMIND ME TO GIVE YOU A RAISE.
ANOTHER ONE?
AT THIS RATE, I'M GOING TO BE MAKING MORE THAN YOU.
TALK. WHO HIRED YOU TO DO THIS?
WHO WAS THIS "WE" YOU WERE REFERRING TO?
THAT? JUST ME, MYSELF, AND I! OR POSSIBLY, ME AND MY SHADOW.
YOU'RE NOT GOING TO TELL ME, ARE YOU?
NOPE. "SABOTEUR/CLIENT PRIVILEGE" IS A MATTER OF PROFESSIONAL PRIDE AMONG US SPYMASTERS.
HOLD UP. THIS IS PEPPER...
YEAH, GIRL, WHAT IS IT? LOOKS LIKE THE CRISIS HAS PASSED--
YOU DON'T SAY...?
GOOD NEWS. LEMON FACE MIGHT NOT HAVE TO TELL US JACK...

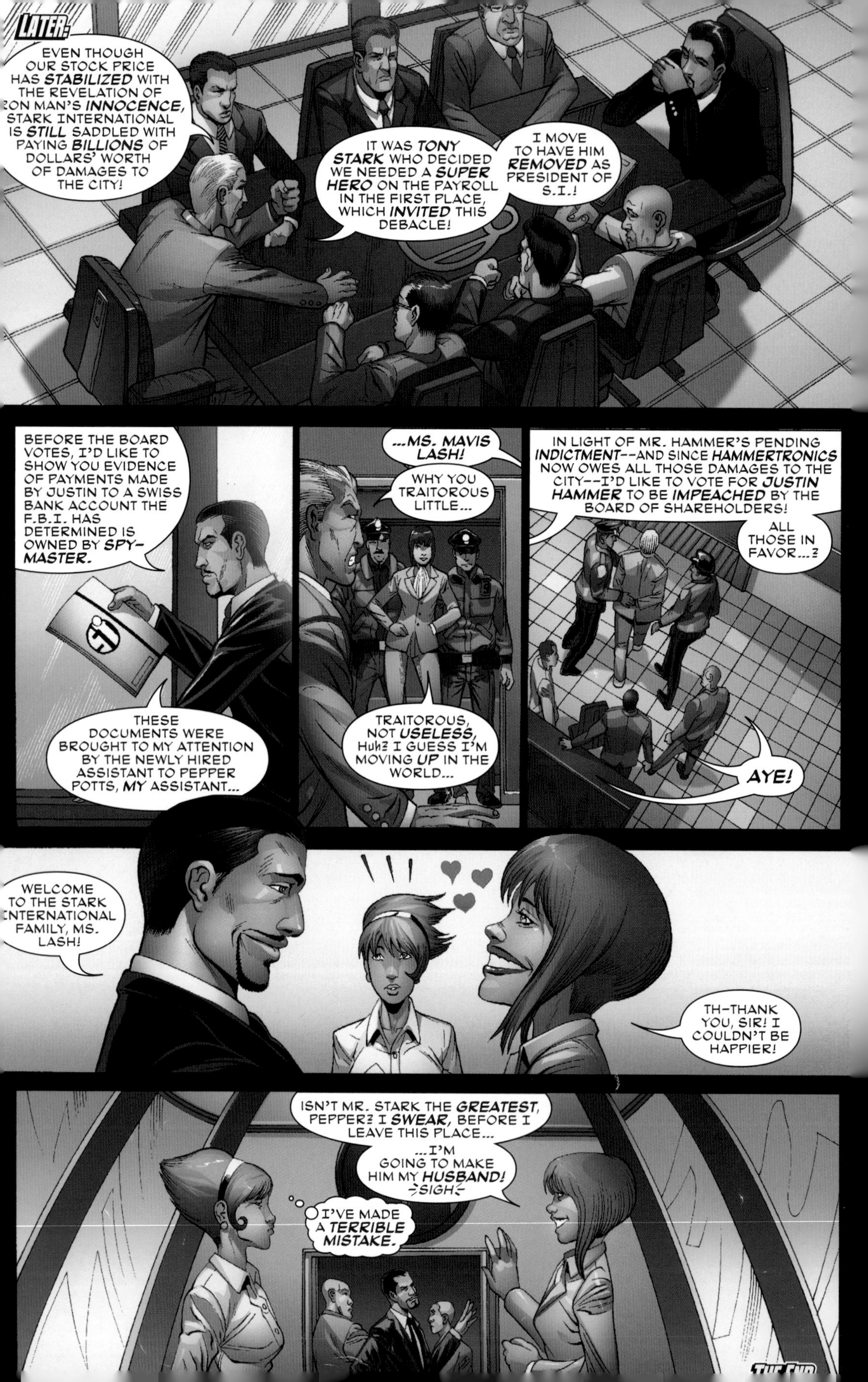
LATER:
EVEN THOUGH OUR STOCK PRICE HAS STABILIZED WITH THE REVELATION OF IRON MAN'S INNOCENCE, STARK INTERNATIONAL IS STILL SADDLED WITH PAYING BILLIONS OF DOLLARS' WORTH OF DAMAGES TO THE CITY!
IT WAS TONY STARK WHO DECIDED WE NEEDED A SUPER HERO ON THE PAYROLL IN THE FIRST PLACE, WHICH INVITED THIS DEBACLE!
I MOVE TO HAVE HIM REMOVED AS PRESIDENT OF S.I.!
BEFORE THE BOARD VOTES, I'D LIKE TO SHOW YOU EVIDENCE OF PAYMENTS MADE BY JUSTIN TO A SWISS BANK ACCOUNT THE F.B.I. HAS DETERMINED IS OWNED BY SPY-MASTER.
THESE DOCUMENTS WERE BROUGHT TO MY ATTENTION BY THE NEWLY HIRED ASSISTANT TO PEPPER POTTS, MY ASSISTANT...
...MS. MAVIS LASH!
WHY YOU TRAITOROUS LITTLE...
TRAITOROUS, NOT USELESS, HUH? I GUESS I'M MOVING UP IN THE WORLD...
IN LIGHT OF MR. HAMMER'S PENDING INDICTMENT--AND SINCE HAMMERTRONICS NOW OWES ALL THOSE DAMAGES TO THE CITY--I'D LIKE TO VOTE FOR JUSTIN HAMMER TO BE IMPEACHED BY THE BOARD OF SHAREHOLDERS!
ALL THOSE IN FAVOR...?
AYE!
WELCOME TO THE STARK INTERNATIONAL FAMILY, MS. LASH!
TH-THANK YOU, SIR! I COULDN'T BE HAPPIER!
ISN'T MR. STARK THE GREATEST, PEPPER? I SWEAR, BEFORE I LEAVE THIS PLACE...
...I'M GOING TO MAKE HIM MY HUSBAND! SIGH
I'VE MADE A TERRIBLE MISTAKE.